SOPHIE TROPHY

To Isabel

Oh-oh! What will Sophie do next?

Eileen Holland

SOPHIE TROPHY

Eileen Holland
Illustrated by Brooke Kerrigan

Library and Archives Canada Cataloguing in Publication
Holland, Eileen, 1955-, author
Sophie Trophy / by Eileen Holland ; Illustrated by Brooke Kerrigan.
Issued in print and electronic formats.
ISBN 978-17753319-3-3 (softcover)
ISBN 978-17753319-8-8 (PDF)
ISBN 978-17753319-7-1 (EPUB)

I. Kerrigan, Brooke, illustrator II. Title.
PS8615.04355S67 2019   jC813'.6
C2018-906372-6   C2018-906400-5

Edited by Jennifer MacKinnon
Copy edited by Dawn Loewen
Proofread by Audrey McClellan
Cover design by Kevin Bertazzon
Interior design by Julia Breese

Published by
Crwth Press
#204 – 2320 Woodland Drive
Vancouver, BC V5N 3P2
778-302-5525

Printed and bound in Canada on 100% post-consumer waste (PCW) paper.

21 20 19 18 · 4 3 2 1

To my husband, Wayne—thank you
for your unwavering belief in me

To my son, Matthew—I will never forget
your words as we walked out of the
library when you were six years old:
"You should write a book, Mommy!"

To my daughter, Kelly—thank you
for revelling in Sophie's simple,
endearing speech and bonding with
her as she came to life on the page

Love to you all

1

PET SPIDER PROBLEMS

The spider flicked its front leg up.

And down.

Up.

And down.

Sophie giggled as she waited by the school door for the morning bell to ring. In her hand was a glass jar. Inside the jar, a spider clung to a twig.

Sophie handed the jar back to Brayden just as their friend Enoli joined them.

"Your pet spider was waving at me, Brayden! Its mother sure taught it good manners."

Brayden's mouth dropped open. "Good manners?"

Sophie grinned. "Yes. It waved hello. I bet it wipes its mouth with a napkin after sucking the blood from its victims, too. And when your spider was a kid? It picked up its toys instead of leaving them all over the web."

Enoli broke into a smile. "Its toys?"

"That's so funny." Brayden let out a snuffly laugh. "Someone should give you a trophy, Sophie, for the goofiest ideas ever."

"Yeah," said a voice behind them. It was Jordy. "Sophie Trophy! That's what I'm going to call you from now on."

Sophie huffed. *Jordy's always trying to embarrass me*, she thought.

The bell rang.

Brayden carefully slipped the spider jar into the side pocket of his backpack.

Sophie, Enoli, and Jordy quietly got into line behind him. Their Grade 3 classmates came running over to join them, laughing and yelling.

Miss Ruby swung the door open. "Good morning! Sophie, Enoli, and Brayden, you may come in. You, too, Jordy. When the rest of you are quiet, you may join them."

"Good morning, Miss Ruby," said Sophie and her friends.

They hurried down the hall to their class.

"Where did you find your spider, Brayden?" Sophie asked as she hung up her coat.

"In my hedge, when I was playing hockey."

Enoli took her library books out of her backpack. "What kind is it?" she asked.

"I'm not sure. I just like how big and round its body is." He took out the jar and slowly spun it to show them.

Sophie's face had a spider-scientist look as she squinted through the glass smudged with fingerprints. "Wow, it really is round. Probably from snacking on all those yummy flies."

Brayden let out another snuffly laugh.

Sophie loved that laugh. It was as if Brayden's nose thought her jokes were funny. He was the first friend she'd made when she came to Hilltop School two months ago. She'd found out right away that he liked her wacky ideas.

Enoli's eyes brightened. "Maybe Miss Ruby will let us look up spiders on the computer."

"Maybe. Let's ask her." Sophie liked how her quiet friend got excited about doing research.

"I'm planning on putting my spider jar on the science table," Brayden said. Then he placed it on the bench along with his hat. He turned to hang his backpack on his hook.

Sophie nodded. "Good idea."

"Hey! What's this?" Jordy stood there, Brayden's jar in one hand and its lid in the other. He was peeking into the jar.

The spider bolted up the twig.

"Watch out, Jordy!" warned Sophie.

"Jordy, no!" cried Brayden.

The spider leaped onto Jordy's nose. It scrambled around one of his nostrils and then around the other. "Get it off me!" He plunked the jar down on the bench and brushed madly at his face.

Sophie blinked. The spider was no longer on Jordy's nose.

It wasn't on the wall.

Or on the floor.

Brayden knelt down to search for it inside a row of shoes. Enoli checked under the bench.

Sophie lifted Brayden's hat. "Where is it?"

Their classmates flooded through the door. Miss Ruby came in with them, her giant earrings swinging. A smile danced on her face. "Where's what?"

"My spider." Brayden sighed. "It got out of its jar."

Miss Ruby rose on tiptoes. "Bray-*den!* You let a spider loose? In here?"

Jordy stomped over to Miss Ruby. "It attacked my nose! I may have to go home sick."

"Lots of legs on spiders, lots of legs," whispered Miss Ruby, her breath ragged.

"Oh ...," said Sophie. It was clear her teacher did not like spiders. Not at all.

But Miss Ruby lifted her head and

squared her shoulders. "Everyone to your seats. Brayden and his friends need room to search for his spider." Waving the last students out of the cloakroom, she hurried after them.

"Oh-oh." Sophie shot a worried-girl look at her friends.

Brayden shook his head. "Double oh-oh."

Sophie and her friends searched the room from top to bottom. But ten minutes later, they still couldn't find the spider. They gave up and told Miss Ruby.

The spider was missing, and so was their teacher's smile.

She kept glancing at the walls.

She kept glancing at the floor.

Sophie imagined Miss Ruby thinking, *Where is that spider?*

2

MISS RUBY IN DANGER

The next morning, Miss Ruby was back to normal. She was teaching about capital letters.

Most of the time, Sophie remembered her capitals. Whenever she did, Miss Ruby would draw a smiley face inside a C (for capital!) on Sophie's page.

Sophie slumped in her seat. When was recess? She loved Miss Ruby, but Sophie's ears were tired of listening.

What if I could make my ears fly off my head? Sophie wondered. She pictured them just flying away. Maybe then her ears could have some real fun. Like listening in on older kids telling secrets. Like overhearing the principal scolding kids running in the hall. Like—

"You're dreaming again, Sophie!"

She lifted her head.

Miss Ruby was standing in front of her.

"Sorry, Miss Ruby." Sophie straightened up in her seat. She didn't want to disappoint her best-teacher-ever. Miss Ruby's I-care smile made her the best. That and her hair.

Miss Ruby had a super-high, puffy ball of brown hair. If she was cheery, it bobbed merrily. If she was tired, it sagged to one side. Some days, it was so tall and fuzzy it reminded Sophie of the cotton candy sold at the summer fair.

Other days, she imagined it was a little animal napping on her teacher's head.

"Hey, Sophie. Stop dreaming!" It was Jordy this time, looking at her from his seat at the next desk.

Sophie frowned at him and tiger-growled under her breath.

"Oooohhh, I'm trembling with fear, Sophie Trophy," Jordy said. He hid his face behind his hands.

Everyone sitting nearby giggled.

Sophie rolled her eyes.

Miss Ruby levelled a stern gaze at him. "That's enough, Jordy."

Sophie looked back at her teacher to show that she was listening. Then something caught her attention.

Something was jiggling above Miss Ruby's hair.

Something that shouldn't be there.

Jiggling.

11

And wiggling.

And quivering.

A round, brown body lowered itself on a silken thread. A brown body attached to eight spindly legs.

A spider was dangling over Miss Ruby's head!

Sophie's tummy turned scared-girl squirmy. A chill ran down her back.

Brayden's spider! She had to warn Miss Ruby.

But then she thought about her friend. Would Brayden get into trouble? He'd brought the spider into the classroom.

The spider dropped lower until it dangled just above Miss Ruby's hair puff.

Sophie clenched her teeth. Should she say something to her teacher?

Miss Ruby stepped over to the white-board. Sophie sighed with relief.

Miss Ruby pointed at a sentence she had written on the board. "Where do the capital letters belong in this sentence, class?"

"On the bank's name," said the boy behind Jordy.

"Good for you." Miss Ruby added the capitals. She stepped back in front of Sophie, right under the spider.

The spider landed in Miss Ruby's hair. It gave all eight of its legs a good, long stretch.

Sophie gulped at the sight. She twisted her lips like gummy worms.

3

SOPHIE IN TROUBLE

Sophie's desk was at the front of the class, by the window.

Miss Ruby, and the spider, stood before her.

The spider could not be seen by the rest of the class.

Not from where they were sitting.

Not on Miss Ruby's brown spider-coloured hair.

Not now that the spider was creeping down the far side of Miss Ruby's head.

Miss Ruby pointed at the same sentence on the board and smiled. "Where do the other capital letters go, Sophie?"

Capital letters? Sophie couldn't think about capital letters when a spider was tiptoeing down her teacher's hair puff.

Suddenly she had an idea. Miss Ruby loved teaching dance. Perhaps a few shakes and spins would send the spider flying. "Shake your head!" Sophie cried. "Shake it! Shake it!"

Miss Ruby froze, her eyes wide. "Pardon me?"

"Your head, Miss Ruby. Shake it! Like this—" Sophie showed her. "And twirl, too. It's fun. Try it!"

The class looked at Sophie as if she were an alien.

"Sophie, we all love to dance, but dance

class is Friday. Right now, we are talking about capital letters. Imagine trying to read a book without them. They let us know when a new sentence is beginning. They tell us which words are names." A smile flickered across Miss Ruby's lips and her eyes glazed over for a moment.

Sophie could tell Miss Ruby loved capital letters.

But the spider! It had come to a stop right above Miss Ruby's ear.

Almost as if it were listening to her.

Almost as if it were thinking about the wonders of capital letters.

Then it stuck a skinny leg forward, like it was trying to decide if it should step onto Miss Ruby's ear.

Sophie felt her breath catch in her throat. She rose out of her chair and pointed. "Your ear! You don't want it on there. Get it off!"

"Get my ear off? You aren't making sense, Sophie." Miss Ruby reached up and patted the hair above her ear. The spider scurried out from under her fingers and crept farther down her head.

Sophie dropped back into her seat. She had to get the spider off her teacher. Leaning across her desk toward Miss Ruby, she cried: "Your head. It's still there. Knock it off!"

"Knock off my head?" In a twinkling, Miss Ruby was at Sophie's desk. She bent down close to her face. "What's going on? You don't seem like yourself at all, Sophie."

The spider was right in front of Sophie's eyes. "Oh, those legs! Up close, they're so hairy!"

Miss Ruby glanced down at her own legs and back up again. "I beg your pardon? My legs aren't hairy!"

The spider crawled onto the collar of Miss Ruby's dress. It pointed a leg at the teacher's giant hoop earring.

"No!" cried Sophie, digging her fingernails into her hands.

The spider leaped onto the earring. It swung back and forth as if it were riding on a playground swing.

Sophie was too upset to laugh. She had to rescue Miss Ruby—and keep Brayden out of trouble. "Whack your ear. That ought to knock it off!"

The class became mouse-quiet.

Sophie grabbed an old test out of her desk and rolled it up. As she swung the test at the spider, Miss Ruby jerked away from her.

"Sophie, I don't know what you think you're doing, but this has to stop." Miss Ruby quick-marched Sophie toward the door. "Go to the principal's office."

"You don't understand, Miss Ruby. There's a spi—"

"Not another word out of you." Miss Ruby snatched the test away. She guided Sophie out the door and shut it firmly.

Now Sophie was the one in trouble.

4

I SPY

Sophie stared at the shut door.

She now felt butterfly-tummy squiggly about the office. And about the unhappy-principal frown she was about to see.

What was the principal's name again?

Her brain kept telling her it was Mr. Homework, but that didn't sound right. Maybe handing out homework was how he punished kids who'd been sent to the office. She hoped not. She didn't like homework.

The hallway ahead of her was long and lonely. It would be scary walking to the office all by herself. She pictured her feet moving bravely forward, step by step, without her.

Sophie felt sorry for her feet.

Sorry.

That was how she felt about Miss Ruby.

Her teacher wasn't happy about the way Sophie had acted. But she didn't deserve to have a spider crawling on her.

What if one of Sophie's classmates saw it and told the rest of the class?

Everyone would stop listening to the teacher.

They would be too busy watching the spider spin a web in her earring.

What if it caught flies?

What if it had babies?

She pictured them creeping across Miss Ruby's face. Poor Miss Ruby. She was already so scared of spiders.

What if ... Sophie sucked in her breath. What if the spider went *inside* Miss Ruby's ear?

Sophie knew she was being silly. But there was just one thing. Her dad always said you look after the people you care about. *And I care about Miss Ruby.* She had to try again.

After checking that no one was in the hallway, Sophie lay down on her tummy. She looked under the classroom door, trying to spot Miss Ruby. All she could see were desk legs and her friends' feet. Brayden's giant runners. Enoli's pink slip-on shoes.

Sophie rolled onto her back and stared at the ceiling. She put on her hardest-thinking look, trying to decide what to do.

Her face squished up like used gum in a wrapper.

An idea sprang into her head. Suddenly she knew just what to do.

First, she would find out if the spider was still on Miss Ruby.

If it wasn't there, *then* she could go to the office.

If it was there, well, she'd have to come up with a new plan.

Sophie ran down the hallway. She always found the outside doors of the school almost too heavy to open. Today, she threw her body against the metal bar. The door swung open so hard it hit the wall.

Running outside, Sophie quietly snuck up below the windows of her classroom. Yet when she stood up, she couldn't see inside. She hopped up and down, but the windows were still too high.

Hearing voices, she turned and saw Brayden and Enoli running toward the playground. Sophie wondered what they were doing.

She glanced up the sidewalk. A diorama box was sticking out of the garbage can. She ran to get it. After placing the box under a window, she stepped onto it.

It flattened to the ground. Groaning, she stepped off.

"Hey, Soph!" Brayden waved as he and Enoli ran toward her.

"Why are you outside?" asked Sophie.

"Miss Ruby just asked for my skating money. I told her it was in my coat pocket, but I left my coat by the swings. She let us come and get it. How come you're out here?"

Sophie felt a sad-heart flutter in her chest. Miss Ruby worried about Brayden and his left-behind coat.

Would she worry about Sophie after today?

Enoli toyed with a button on her jacket. "Aren't you supposed to be at the office, Sophie?"

"I'm trying to see if the spider is still on Miss Ruby's earring."

Enoli's lips twisted downward. "A spider? On her earring?"

Brayden's eyebrows lifted. "Oh, no."

Sophie bit her lip. "Yes, Brayden, it might be your spider. I was afraid to tell Miss Ruby. You might get into trouble."

"She's scared of spiders," said Enoli.

"Is she ever!" An idea popped into Sophie's head. "Brayden, can I stand on your back?"

Brayden smiled. "Yeah, sure." Dropping his coat, he got down on his hands and knees.

Grabbing Enoli's shoulder, Sophie

rose up on shaky spy-girl legs until she was just high enough to peek inside the window. There was a lump on Miss Ruby's earring. "It's still there!"

"What's still there?" asked a gruff voice.

Sophie and her friends screamed.

They fell in a pile below the window.

Sophie looked up out of the tangle of arms and legs.

She saw what no kid at school wants to see.

The principal.

5

JORDY CHICKENS OUT

Sophie got to her feet. She heard voices overhead and looked up.

The class must have heard their screams.

Everyone was staring out the windows.

Jordy opened a window and stuck his head out. "Hey, it's Sophie Trophy!"

Someone near him snickered.

Jordy again, thought Sophie. She

wished she could dig a hole in the ground and hide in it.

Miss Ruby appeared at the window. She clapped her hands. "Class, back to your seats. Class!"

Nobody listened. Half the kids were staring out the windows. The other half were hopping up and down behind them, trying to see who'd screamed.

Miss Ruby bent down to look out the window. "Sophie, what are you doing outside?"

Sophie held her breath. Miss Ruby's earring was dangling right in front of Jordy. If he saw the spider, he might help Miss Ruby.

The spider ran back and forth along the lower curve of the earring, enough to start it swinging again.

Jordy pulled away from the spider. "Eww."

I should have known he'd be too scared to help. Sophie curled her fists angry-girl tightly. "Do something, Jordy!"

Jordy covered his eyes. "I can't look."

"Miss Ruby's earring," she cried. "Flick your finger. Knock it off."

There was a gasp from above. Sophie didn't need to look up to know that she had disappointed Miss Ruby. Again.

Mr. Homework frowned. "What did you say?"

Sophie didn't have time to think about how her behaviour looked to her new principal. She had to act quickly, but he was blocking her path. So were Brayden and Enoli. There was only one way out.

She scooted between the principal's legs.

"Hey!" he shouted, but Sophie was gone.

She pulled open the door and raced down the hallway to the classroom.

Miss Ruby and the class were still at the windows.

Darting over to the science table, Sophie grabbed the fishnet lying beside the aquarium. Heart pounding, she edged toward her teacher.

As Sophie lifted the net, Miss Ruby turned. "What are you doing?"

It was time for Sophie to tell her about the spider.

But first she had to catch the spider with the net. Because if her teacher found out she had a spider on her ...

Sophie pictured Miss Ruby doing an icky-bug dance as she tried to get the spider off.

She would be batting at her head with both hands.

Her hair puff would flop from side to side.

The whole class would watch.

34

Everyone would know that she was scared.

Just thinking about it, Sophie felt pain in her heart for Miss Ruby.

"Your head. I have to get it off."

"That's enough, Sophie!" Miss Ruby's hand darted out. She grabbed the handle of the net. Her sudden movement sent the spider flying.

It landed on its back in the net. Then it did a crazy upside-down dance until it got on its feet again.

Success! Sophie whirled around, ready to take the spider to its jar.

Instead, she bumped headfirst into a striped brown suit.

A large hand took the net away from Sophie.

And the net's spider passenger.

Sophie looked up.

It was Mr. Homework. He was wearing

the unhappy-principal frown. "Come with me."

He set the net down and marched Sophie out the door.

Oh-oh, she thought.

She had missed her chance to tell Miss Ruby about the spider.

6

ELEPHANTS
IN THE OFFICE

Sophie wiggled in her chair.

The office was grownup-quiet. Sophie got the scream-loudly feeling.

On the other side of a high counter sat the secretary.

The phone rang.

Ms. Babette answered it.

All Sophie could see was Ms. Babette's hair and the pencil stuck behind her ear.

"Oh, I quite agree. You are so right," said Ms. Babette, pulling the pencil out. "Let me just write that down, then. Uh-huh … uh-huh … uh-huh." She put the pencil back behind her ear. "Oh, yes, yes, yes, yes."

Sophie watched the pencil bounce as the secretary nodded. She imagined the pencil talking on the phone on its own.

No Ms. Babette eyes.

No Ms. Babette nose and mouth.

No Ms. Babette body.

Just the pencil.

The door of the principal's office opened. Enoli and Brayden walked past. They looked pale.

Sophie's lower lip trembled.

She wanted to run after them.

She wanted to say she was sorry they had to talk to the principal.

She picked at a loose thread on her

pants. It reminded her of the spider dangling above Miss Ruby. *Miss Ruby, my best-teacher-ever. Miss Ruby, who thinks I'm rude.*

Sophie sadly looped the thread around her finger and snapped it off. She watched it glide to the floor.

There was an eraser under her chair. Some kid had probably dropped it. Some kid sent to do his work in the office because he talked too much in class.

Sophie pictured him sitting in the chair, adding numbers. She saw the eraser slip off his lap.

Sophie felt sorry for the boy. He had lost his eraser.

She felt sorry for the eraser. It had lost its boy.

She looked up. Ms. Babette's pencil was still nodding.

Sophie slid snake-girl smoothly under

her chair and grabbed the eraser. It had a hole in it. The talking-too-much kid must have drilled it with his pencil.

Every eraser she owned had a drill hole. Or two.

Three even.

Sometimes she played with her erasers so much, her teacher took them away from her.

Sophie peeked through the eraser hole. *Hey, it's like using Dad's special camera,* she thought.

She imagined herself sneaking up on a herd of elephants.

In Africa.

On a safari.

Dust rose with every step the elephants took.

Sophie thought for a moment. *Wild elephants are dangerous. I'd better hide.*

She tugged her sweatshirt off. It

was hard to do quietly under a chair. Especially with a nodding pencil nearby.

Sticking her head inside it, she looked out the neck hole.

The office disappeared.

Ms. Babette and the pencil disappeared.

Sophie was in the grasslands of Africa.

The elephants were walking toward her.

She looked through the eraser hole. "*Click!* Sophie, the world-famous wildlife photographer, snaps a picture of the elephants' tusks. *Click!* She takes a picture of a baby elephant holding on to its mother's tail. *Click!* She snaps a shot of ... of..."

Pant legs?

One pair of striped pants with shiny principal shoes below.

One pair of polka-dot pants with pointy secretary shoes below.

Sophie dropped the eraser.

She pulled her head out of the sweatshirt.

Mr. Homework and Ms. Babette were standing in front of her.

Their arms were crossed.

Their eyebrows were scrunched down low on their foreheads.

Too low.

Mr. Homework uncrossed his arms. "Come into my office, young lady."

Sophie didn't feel like taking pictures of elephants anymore. She crawled out from under the chair. She didn't even slide out snake-girl smoothly.

7

SOPHIE TO THE RESCUE

The recess bell rang as Sophie took a seat across from Mr. Homework.

She hated missing recess. But not as much as she hated disappointing Miss Ruby. This had to be the worst day ever.

Mr. Homework leaned forward in his chair. "Let's talk about why you were outside, Sophie."

"I was trying to help Miss Ruby. There was a spi—"

Ms. Babette poked her head through the doorway. "Excuse me, but there's a stray dog chasing the students around the field. Three children just came in crying. They fell down running away from it."

Mr. Homework stood up. "Miss Ruby told me what happened in the classroom, Sophie. While I'm gone, please think about your behaviour." He walked out.

Sophie sighed. She stared around the room.

Important principal papers were stacked beside Mr. Homework's computer. There was a photo of Mr. Homework when he was young. An older man had his arm around the principal. Sophie had never thought about principal-dads before.

A sunbeam was shining on something under the desk.

It glowed like treasure.

It was a gold-all-over pen.

Sophie pictured Mr. Homework searching his pockets for the pen. She imagined him looking through his desk. She had a sad-girl feeling about Mr. Homework's missing pen.

Dropping to her knees, Sophie reached for the pen. Sitting up, she rolled it over. There were words on it. *To my son on his first day of teaching.* Mr. Homework's dad must have given him the pen a long time ago.

Sophie pressed the top of the pen.

Click! The pen's tip came out, ready for writing.

Click! It went back in again.

Sophie unscrewed the pen. A spring inside made the pen's tip go in and out. She pictured herself on a giant spring, hopping through the schoolyard. *Sproing! Sproing! Sproing!*

The kids would stop playing soccer. They'd come to see her from every corner of the playground. "There goes Sophie," they'd say. "She saved Miss Ruby from a spider."

As Sophie raised her hand to do a queen wave at them, she remembered she was in the principal's office. There were voices outside the window. She slipped over to peek out.

It was Enoli and Brayden.

She opened the window. "I'm sorry you guys had to go to the office."

"It's okay," said Enoli. "Are you in trouble?"

Sophie leaned out the window, screwing and unscrewing the pen. "I don't know. We haven't talked yet. What did you tell the principal?"

"About leaving my coat outside," said Brayden. "And you standing on my back."

"Did you tell him about the spider?"

"No." Enoli looked at the ground.

Sophie's eyes widened. "Why not?"

"He didn't ask," said Enoli. "It's scary in the principal's office. All I said was a bunch of yeses and nos."

"Me, too," Brayden said. "I didn't want him to know it was my spider on Miss Ruby."

"I don't blame you," said Sophie.

The end-of-recess bell rang.

"Brayden?"

"Yeah, Soph?"

Her stomach twisted. "I kinda have to tell the principal about the spider."

Brayden swished his shoe through the puddle below the window. "Yeah, I know." he said. "Just tell him it wasn't me who let it loose."

Sophie nodded. She watched Enoli and Brayden walk away.

Mr. Homework was taking so long. She clicked the top of his pen.

Nothing happened.

Sophie clicked again.

Its tip didn't come out.

She unscrewed the pen.

The spring was gone!

She looked down. Something shiny was in the puddle.

"Oh, no!" Sophie had to fix Mr. Homework's gold-all-over pen or he couldn't sign important principal papers. He couldn't order hot lunches or buy new computers and gym balls.

Jordy ran past the window.

"Jordy," she called, "can you get that spring out of the puddle?"

"What? I'm not helping you, Sophie Trophy." He ran off, twirling his arms like propellers on a plane.

Sophie groaned.

She would have to get the spring back herself.

She screwed the gold-all-over pen back together and placed it on Mr. Homework's desk. Then she looked around the room. A hockey stick was leaning in the corner.

Sophie lowered the stick out the window toward the puddle. It didn't reach far enough.

Spotting a basket filled with school T-shirts, she removed the shirts, flipped the basket over, and stepped up on it. Sophie inched her tummy over the windowsill. She scooped the curved blade of the hockey stick right under the spring.

Success!

Suddenly, Sophie fell forward. The hockey stick went flying as her legs flipped into the air.

Before she could hit the ground, she was jerked to a stop. Her foot was caught on something. As she dangled there, Sophie looked back over her shoulder and groaned. Her shoelace was looped over the window latch!

Sophie was so close to the spring. She stretched her fingers toward it, but the ground was out of reach. She tried to free her shoe again and again, grunting loudly. Sophie's struggles only made her swing back and forth wildly. It was no use.

She felt like a spider hanging on a thread.

Sophie heard footsteps inside the principal's office. "What on earth?" said a deep, grumpy voice.

She felt a jolt as her shoelace gave way. "NO!"

8

PUDDLE MUDDLE

Sophie lifted her face out of the puddle. Dirty water streamed down her shirt.

She blinked.

"Are you all right?" called Mr. Homework from above.

She swished her fingers through the puddle until she felt something thin and firm. Sophie rose to her knees and waved the spring at him. "I got it back! I saved

Hot Lunch Day! I saved the new computers and gym balls!"

Unhappy-principal lines wrinkled Mr. Homework's forehead. He tipped his head to the side and frowned. "Why are you outside?"

She lowered her arm. "I was getting the spring. Plus, I need to tell you about the scary, hairy-legged—"

"Sophie, I don't understand what's going on right now, but we need to get you cleaned up. Go change into your gym clothes. Then come and see me."

Sophie's shoulders sagged. Wobbling to her feet, she headed back into the school. As she walked down the hall, she thought about Miss Ruby's I-care smile. *Miss Ruby won't be smiling at me anymore. Not when she hears I was hanging upside down outside the principal's window.*

Sophie sighed.

She smelled like a mud puddle.

She looked like one, too.

Sophie didn't want Miss Ruby or the class to see her like this.

Opening the classroom door quiet-girl softly, she peeked inside.

Miss Ruby was teaching about the helping members in a community.

Sophie wished she was in her seat listening to the lesson. She loved hearing about police officers catching bad guys. About driving a car with flashing lights and a siren. Sophie would keep the siren on all day long if she were an officer.

Miss Ruby was talking about firefighters, too. About saving people and pets in burning houses. Sophie would save dogs and cats if she were a firefighter. Goldfish in bowls, too.

Pet spiders even.

When Miss Ruby turned her back, Sophie tiptoed into the cloakroom and grabbed her gym bag. If she could slip out unnoticed, she could head straight to the washroom to change her clothes.

"It's so nice out," said Miss Ruby. "Let's go outside for gym. Jordy, will you please get the box of skipping ropes from the cloakroom?"

Oh-oh! Sophie heard feet shuffling across the room. She had seconds to hide.

Her coat hung on a hook beside her. Kneeling on the bench, Sophie shoved her head and body inside her coat. She reached an arm out, grabbed Brayden's coat, and flung it over her legs.

Sophie crossed her fingers. For added luck, she looped her big toes over her second toes, squeezing tightly.

Jordy sprinted past.

She heard cardboard shifting and skipping-rope handles rattling. Jordy groaned. "How can skipping ropes be so heavy?"

Something bashed into Sophie's legs.

There was screaming, then a crash.

Sophie shoved her coat aside.

Jordy was on the floor with the box on his head, clawing at the tangle of skipping ropes in front of his eyes. "Help! Brayden's spider caught me in its web!"

Miss Ruby rushed into the cloakroom. She pulled the ropes off Jordy. "What happened?"

Looking over his shoulder, Jordy spotted Sophie rubbing her legs. "First, Sophie gets Brayden's spider to attack me. Then she trips me!"

"I'm sorry," said Sophie. "I didn't mean to."

Miss Ruby glanced at Sophie. "I hope not."

Sophie's cheeks burned.

If only her gym bag was bigger. She would hide inside it and never come out.

9

THE PRINCIPAL'S OFFICE

After changing into her gym clothes, Sophie headed to the office.

Mr. Homework was busy with a visitor when she arrived. Sophie sat down to wait.

Ms. Babette was on the phone. Her pencil wasn't nodding this time. It was shaking from side to side. "Oh, don't tell me. How terrible! No, no, no, no. If that poor girl fell off her pony, you must keep her at home another day, math test or not." Ms. Babette's pencil kept shaking, even after she stopped talking.

Sophie felt dizzy watching it.

Mr. Homework's voice made a blurry buzz behind his door. His throat would be sore after all that talking. Perhaps he would have to go home sick. Then Sophie would be excused from speaking with him.

The lunch bell rang.

Mr. Homework's visitor left. Sophie's stomach rumbled as she walked into the principal's office.

Familiar footsteps entered the outer office. It was Miss Ruby.

"I invited Miss Ruby to hear what you have to say, Sophie," explained Mr. Homework as they sat down.

Sophie took a brave-girl breath. "Miss Ruby, I was trying hard to listen to you

this morning. I only yelled 'shake it' to help you."

Mr. Homework frowned. "Is it polite to yell at your teacher and interrupt her lesson?"

"No. But I wanted her to shake the spider off."

"The spider?" Miss Ruby raised her fingertips to her lips.

"Yes. It landed in your hair and crawled down above your ear." Sophie's nose scrunched up like a lump of playdough.

Miss Ruby closed her eyes, shivered, and opened them again.

"Why didn't you just tell Miss Ruby about the spider, Sophie?" Mr. Homework asked

Sophie bumped her heel softly against her chair leg. "Because it might just be ..." The rest of her words came out in a rush. "... Brayden's pet spider. I was afraid

Brayden would get into trouble," she said.

Mr. Homework raised his eyebrows.

"It escaped in the cloakroom yester-day," explained Miss Ruby.

"Yes, after someone let it out of Brayden's jar." Sophie bumped her heel against her chair again. "I had to get the spider off you, Miss Ruby. You thought I was trying to hurt you, but I would never do that. When you sent me to the office, I ran outside—"

Mr. Homework nodded. "—and stood on Brayden's back—"

"—to see if the spider was still on you. What if it spun a web in your earring? Or crept inside your ear ..." Sophie covered her own ear, scared-girl tightly. She wasn't surprised to see Miss Ruby do the same.

"I was shocked at how you acted this morning, Sophie," Miss Ruby said. She tilted her head, thinking. "I understand now that you wanted to help me and you wanted to protect Brayden. That was an uncomfortable situation."

"I didn't know what to do." Sophie jerked her shoulders up, then down again.

"Sometimes it's difficult to help one person without hurting another," said Miss Ruby.

Mr. Homework pressed his lips together. "Hmm. So, why were you hanging upside down outside my window?"

"Upside down?" Miss Ruby blinked several times.

Sophie glanced at the principal, her cheeks flaming hot. "I found your dad-pen on the floor when I was waiting for you. I just had to hold it. By accident, I dropped its spring out the window.

"I couldn't leave the pen all wrecked. When I tried to scoop up the spring with a hockey stick, I fell out the window."

"Oh, goodness me." Miss Ruby gripped the armrests of her chair.

"My shoelace got caught on the window latch, so I hung there until it let go. I fell in the puddle."

Mr. Homework shook his head. "You're lucky you didn't hurt yourself!"

Sophie took the spring out of her pocket. "May I fix your pen, please?"

Mr. Homework handed it to her.

Sophie opened the pen, snapped the spring back into place, then screwed the pen shut.

She clicked the pen tip out.

And in.

Out.

And in.

Out.

And in.

"Okay, okay, Sophie. The pen works." Mr. Homework took it away from her.

"And Jordy?" asked Miss Ruby.

"I was getting my gym bag to change into clean clothes. I was all muddy, so I didn't want Jordy to see me, and I hid. He tripped over me when he was carrying the skipping ropes. I said I was sorry," said Sophie, her voice trembling. "I am sorry, Mr. Homework."

The principal frowned. "Mr. Homework? That's not my name."

Sophie drew back. "It isn't?"

"No. My name is Mr. Homewood."

"Oh. I kinda got mixed up."

"Yes," said Mr. Homewood. "Just like everyone got mixed up about what you were doing. It's good that you care about your teacher, Sophie, but your imagination got you in trouble today. Perhaps you can use it differently."

Sophie's eyebrows squished together as she thought. "In a helping way? Or in a smart-thinking way?"

The lines in the principal's forehead softened. "That's up to you, Sophie."

Miss Ruby nodded. "You'll figure it out."

10

SOPHIE TROPHY, SPIDER EXPERT

Sophie sat in the classroom and ate lunch while Miss Ruby finished some marking.

She nibbled at her sandwich. She was still worried about the spider. What if it was hiding somewhere in the classroom, feeling lost and scared? Suddenly an idea popped into her head. Maybe she could use her imagination to help find it.

She looked around the room, trying to think about where she would hide if she were a spider.

The windowsills. Miss Ruby's cactus. The science table, with its bouquet of autumn leaves, its robin's nest, its aquarium, and its fishnet. She wondered if the spider had noticed the fishnet's web-like pattern. Just looking at it would make the little critter long for its webby home in Brayden's hedge.

Sophie imagined the spider with tears in its eyes.

Sophie teared up, too, just thinking about it.

When she finished eating, Sophie walked over to Miss Ruby's desk. Maybe if she knew more about the spider, she would know how to find it. "May I please research spiders on the class computer? With Brayden and Enoli?"

"Yes, you may. Perhaps you can figure out if Brayden's spider is dangerous."

"We'll try." Sophie hurried out to the playground. She signalled to Enoli and Brayden to come inside.

Enoli sat down at the computer with Sophie and Brayden on either side of her. She started by researching spiders that lived in their area. "Wow, there are more than seven hundred kinds. Hobo spiders, zebra jumpers, tarantulas—"

"Tarantulas? Wow." Sophie smiled.

"—wolf spiders, orb weavers—"

"Wait!" Brayden squinted at a photo on the screen. "That might be my spider! The cross orb weaver."

"It might be."

"Orb weavers have white dots on their backs in the shape of a cross," read Enoli. "Although they have eight eyes, their eyesight is poor. They know they've caught something in their web by feeling the vibrations."

"Plus, their webs are wheel-shaped, like the one in my hedge," added Brayden.

Enoli scrolled farther down the page. "Grass spiders, house spiders, western black widows—"

Sophie lifted her hand. "Look what it says. 'The western black widow can deliver a painful bite, with discomfort that lasts for days.'"

"We must make sure that your spider isn't a western black widow," said Miss Ruby.

The three friends continued research-ing until the bell rang.

The class streamed in from the play-ground, turning the quiet room lively.

When everyone was seated, Miss Ruby's I-care smile lit up her face. "No wonder Sophie was so upset this morning," she said. "She was trying to warn me that a spider was on my head!"

Gasps rose from the students.

Miss Ruby shivered. "The thought of that spider landing on me!"

"Yeah," called out Jordy, a smile plastered across his face, "with all eight of its legs!"

The class giggled.

Miss Ruby rolled her eyes and smiled. "Please give me your poetry projects before you line up to go to the library. Sophie, your row is first to go."

Yes! First to go! If I'm quick, I can search for spider hideaways before we leave, Sophie thought. The sound of papers rustling and chairs scraping the floor filled the room.

Sophie handed in her homework. Then she scooted around, checking the locations she had imagined at lunchtime.

The windowsills.

Nothing.

Miss Ruby's cactus.

Nothing.

The science table.

Sophie searched between the bottles near the aquarium.

"What are you doing, Soph?" asked Brayden as he and Enoli walked up.

"Looking for your spider."

Jordy popped up on the far side of the science table. His fingers were spread spider-leg spookily above his head. He had paper spider fangs taped over his mouth. He called out, "Suddenly, Brayden's spider became the size of a human!"

Sophie, Enoli, and Brayden gasped and stumbled backward.

Enoli pressed her hands against her cheeks. "You scared me!"

Jordy laughed. "I scared *all* of you. Even Sophie Trophy!"

Sophie frowned. "Stop calling me that, Jordy."

"Why? It's funny."

"Not if you say it to be mean," said Sophie.

"Yeah, Jordy." Brayden frowned. "I said she should get a trophy because she has the funniest ideas. She thinks up interesting things."

Enoli nodded. "Sophie thinks a lot. I like that."

"See, Jordy? I would be happy if Brayden and Enoli called me Sophie Trophy."

Jordy stuck out his chin. "All right, I get it."

When Sophie returned to her spider search, something seemed different.

The cheery-looking fish that was

pictured on the fish food bottle looked strange.

Like it was wearing a scarf.

When the scarf started creeping down the bottle, Sophie giggled and pointed at it. "Look!"

Brayden drew in his breath. "My spider!"

Enoli grinned. "You found it."

"Yes! I figured the spider would go to the science table to be near nature's things."

As they watched, the spider stepped onto the table. It crept over to a leaf that had fallen from the autumn bouquet and disappeared inside its curled edge.

Sophie couldn't help smiling.

Jordy reached their side of the table, looked around, then glared at her. He waved his arms. "The spider isn't here. You're tricking me, Sophie."

Jordy's hand bumped two bottles.

They fell over, knocking the leaf to the floor.

Sophie's mouth dropped open. "Jordy, the spider was hiding in the leaf! We'll never catch it now that it's on the floor."

"On the floor?" He squatted and peered at the leaf.

The spider left its hiding place. It raced toward Jordy, its legs a blur.

Jordy flopped backward onto the floor. He bum-bumped away from the spider before turning and scrambling to his feet. Pushing several classmates aside, he plowed through the lineup at the door. "Brayden's spider is chasing me! Run!"

The screams of his classmates cut through the air.

11

GOODBYE,
LITTLE FRIEND

"Brayden's spider?" Miss Ruby looked up from collecting homework.

"Yes!" cried a girl at the back of the lineup. She grabbed her friend's arm and they ran toward the hallway.

Half of the kids in the lineup ran after them. The other half tried to catch the spider or cheered on their friends who were chasing it.

The spider ran circles around their feet. Like a figure skater doing spins.

Like a mountain biker on a winding trail.

Brayden shook his head. "My poor spider. Somebody's going to step on it."

Enoli handed Brayden the jar. "Not if you catch it."

As Brayden hurried after the spider, one of his giant runners caught on a desk leg. He nose-dived to the floor, and the jar rolled out of his hand.

It was up to Sophie now. Hoping that Miss Ruby would forgive her, she called out, "Brayden's spider will be safer if you all go out in the hallway!"

"You're quite right, Sophie," said Miss Ruby. Sophie's classmates stopped charging around and tiptoed carefully out the door. Miss Ruby followed them, her eyes watchful.

Sophie noticed Jordy at Miss Ruby's

side, watching from the doorway. Was he worried about the spider getting hurt?

She found the spider under a baseball mitt below a desk. It was a peaceful hide-away after dodging all those feet.

Sophie imagined the spider fanning itself with two of its eight legs.

Wiping its brow with a handkerchief.

Chug-a-lugging a glass of water.

Creeping up on her sneaky spider-catcher feet, Sophie knelt down behind the mitt.

Brayden scuffed across the floor as quietly as he could in his giant runners. He passed her the jar.

She unscrewed the lid and lifted the mitt.

Plunk! She slipped the jar over the spider. "I got it!"

When the spider scrambled partway up the glass, Sophie tipped the jar to one side. She screwed the lid into place and turned the jar upright.

Brayden and Enoli waved their arms and cheered. Miss Ruby clapped her hands as she came back in the room.

Sophie handed the spider jar to Brayden.

"Thanks, Soph."

There was a whoop from the doorway, and Jordy dashed inside. "Now I have a good reason to call you Sophie Trophy. You deserve one because you are brave, you care about spiders, and you are the best spider catcher ever."

Sophie giggled. "If that's why you want to call me Sophie Trophy, then go ahead, Jordy."

"Yes!" He ran back out the door, both arms raised high above his head.

Sophie and her friends laughed.

"Jordy's right," said Miss Ruby. "You

were my hero today when you protected me. Now you are the spider's hero, too!"

Brave-girl feelings tickled Sophie's insides. "Thank you."

"Have you figured out yet if it's a western black widow?" asked Miss Ruby.

"Let's check," said Enoli. "The western black widow has a red, hourglass-shaped mark on its abdomen."

Sophie lifted the jar so they could look at the spider from underneath.

Enoli grinned. "It doesn't have one."

Sophie giggled. "And it isn't black, either!"

"Oh, what good news!" Miss Ruby leaned back against her desk. She let her breath out slowly.

"It has a cross on its back," said Brayden. "Like the photo we saw of the orb weaver."

Enoli nodded. "A cross of white dots

and a round abdomen. The website said that orb weavers are most noticeable in the fall when the females get bigger as they prepare for breeding."

"Its big, round body is what you liked about it, Brayden," said Sophie.

"It's the big, round web that it's named after," said Miss Ruby, peering over their shoulders.

Sophie and her friends turned their heads to look at their teacher.

Miss Ruby chuckled. Her hair puff jiggled as if it were chuckling, too. "What you were reading earlier was interesting. I couldn't help listening. An orb is a ball, circle, or wheel, or something shaped like one. Just this morning, I saw an orb weaver's web in a bush by my front door. It was pretty, all covered in dew."

Sophie and her friends smiled.

Miss Ruby sighed. "Spiders move so

quickly. When I see one, I just want to run away!"

"We found out that most spiders are harmless, Miss Ruby," said Enoli. "If they feel threatened, they run away or hide or camouflage themselves."

"They feel exactly the way you feel!" said Sophie. "Most of them are as gentle as the spider in *Charlotte's Web*. And Charlotte was an orb weaver!"

"Really? I always liked Charlotte." Miss Ruby smiled. "Brayden, what are you going to do with your spider?"

Brayden shrugged. "Spiders can't catch flies in jars, can they? I guess I've got to find my little friend a new home."

"Good idea, Brayden. Why don't you three go outside and look for one? You can meet us at the library when you are done." Miss Ruby slipped out into the hallway.

Sophie pointed at a red-twig dogwood bush outside. "That bush would be a happy home for a spider."

Brayden smiled. "It sure would."

Brayden and Enoli and Sophie headed outside.

When they reached the bush, Brayden handed the jar to Sophie. A sigh escaped his throat. "You saved my spider, Soph. You should be the one to put it in its new home."

"He's right, Sophie," said Enoli.

Sophie had a happy-heart feeling about her friends. She unscrewed the lid from the jar and tipped the spider out onto a branch.

Brayden leaned toward the bush, his eyelids crinkling at the edges. "Goodbye, little friend."

The spider ran in jiggly circles before crawling away along the branch.

Sophie laughed. "Did your spider just do a happy dance, Brayden?"

"I guess it did!" Brayden let out a snuffly laugh.

After school, Sophie and her friends headed out to look for the spider.

Something glistened between the branches of the dogwood bush.

Brayden's eyes widened. "My spider's spinning a web."

"It seems cheerful, doesn't it?" said Sophie.

Enoli nodded. "Yes, it does."

Placing her hands on her friends' shoulders, Sophie asked, "Do you think the spider will do a happy dance when it finishes the web?"

Brayden and Enoli laughed.

Sophie couldn't wait to see the web the next morning with her friends.

And maybe even with Miss Ruby.

ACKNOWLEDGEMENTS

Heartfelt thanks to my WriteonFest colleagues, not only for their editing expertise, but for their devotion to Sophie and that skedaddling spider: Karen Autio, Pat Fraser, Loraine Kemp, and Mary Ann Thompson. Thank you as well to Fiona Bayrock and Sharon Helberg for their early assistance. Thanks to Eileen Kernaghan and the Kyle Centre Writer's Group in Port Moody, for their invaluable critiquing. Thanks also to my students at Ranch Park Elementary, who buoyed me up by laughing in the right places as I read to them.

I felt sheer delight when I saw Brooke Kerrigan's illustrations of the characters in *Sophie Trophy*. How fortunate I am that she agreed to illustrate the book. Many thanks go to substantive editor Jennifer MacKinnon and copy editor Dawn Loewen, for the opportunity to benefit from their remarkable editing skills. Kevin Bertazzon and Julia Breese, I appreciate the attractive book layout and design. I am grateful to Diane Morriss of Sono Nis Press for not only believing in *Sophie Trophy*, but for taking a chance on a debut children's book author. I'm glad she chose publisher Melanie Jeffs of Crwth Press to finish the book's publication, as Melanie's respectful demeanour, efficiency, and unique flair for promotion make working with her a pleasure.

My family has supported me in countless ways. I thank Wayne, Matthew, and

Kelly for their encouragement. It kept me writing.

Lastly, thanks to the two Ranch Park students who called out a frantic warning as I was teaching many years ago, when a spider tried to lower itself into my hair.

ABOUT THE AUTHOR

Eileen Holland is a former teacher who lives in Coquitlam, British Columbia. Eileen spent her early school years letting her imagination spin her away from the classroom. It is not too much of a stretch to imagine her creating a dreamy character like Sophie Trophy for her first book.

Learn more about Eileen Holland and *Sophie Trophy* at www.EileenHollandChildrensAuthor.com.

ABOUT CRWTH PRESS

Crwth (pronounced *crooth*) Press is a small independent publisher based in British Columbia. A crwth is a Welsh stringed instrument that was commonly played until the 1800s, when it was replaced by the violin. We chose this word for the company name because we like the way music brings people together, and we want our press to do the same.

Crwth Press is committed to sustainability and accessibility. This book is printed in Canada on 100 percent post-consumer waste paper using only vegetable-based inks. For more on our sustainability efforts, visit www.crwth.ca.

To make our books accessible, we use fonts that individuals with dyslexia find easier to read. The font for this book is Lexie Readable.

LOOKING FOR MORE BOOKS ABOUT EXCEPTIONAL GIRLS?

Check out *Isobel's Stanley Cup* by Kristin Butcher.

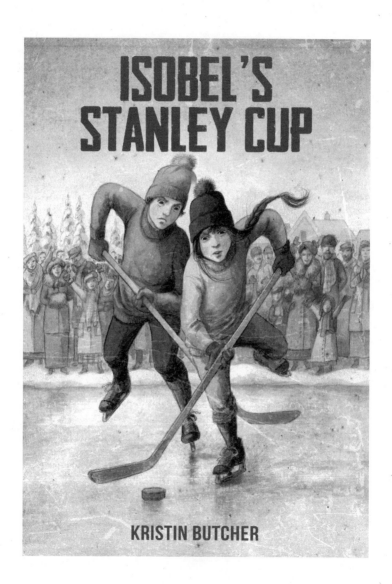

ISOBEL'S
STANLEY CUP

KRISTIN BUTCHER

ABOUT *ISOBEL'S STANLEY CUP* BY KRISTIN BUTCHER

More than anything, Isobel Harkness wants to play hockey with her older brothers. But it's 1893, and a lot of people—including her father—think hockey is only for boys.

Ignoring her father's wishes, Isobel helps her brothers train for an upcoming game. And she begins to shine on the ice. When she meets Isobel Stanley, one of the first women to play hockey, young Isobel gets some great advice.

When Isobel has a chance to skate in a big game with the best of the boys in her neighbourhood, she has to find a way around her father's rules.

Inspired by true accounts of Isobel Stanley's role in the history of hockey, *Isobel's Stanley Cup* proves that hockey has always been a game for girls.

PAPA SAYS NO

Isobel circled the dining table, banging down knives and forks and throwing the napkins onto the plates. She could hear her brothers in the other room. She could smell them too. Well, not them, exactly. But she could smell the fresh winter air they had brought indoors after their snowball fight.

She had watched them through the window as she'd dusted the sitting room.

It looked like such fun. She had wanted to play too. But according to Papa, throwing snowballs wasn't a suitable activity for a young lady. Neither was hockey, and Isobel wanted to do that more than anything.

She hated having to be a young lady. It was boring. Boys had all the fun.

Isobel might have been happier if she'd had a sister to do things with. But she didn't. All she had were five brothers. To make matters worse, they were all older.

She sighed. All she ever got to do was help her mother with chores. It was so unfair. She didn't want to embroider pillow slips and fold laundry. She wanted to play hockey with her brothers.

As she put out the water glasses, she made her mind up. She would ask Papa one more time.

———•———

Isobel glared at the newspaper hiding her father's face.

"It's not fair!" She pouted.

Mama shook her head in warning, and Isobel's brothers stopped eating. Their eyes bugged out as they stared at their little sister. No one ever spoke back to Papa.

Papa lowered his *Ottawa Citizen* and put it down beside his plate. Then he took off his spectacles and laid them down too.

He frowned at Isobel. "The world is not always fair, Isobel. You will find that out soon enough. But this is not about fairness. It's about what is proper. Some activities are meant for boys and some for girls. It's as simple as that. Hockey is a boys' game. It is not suitable for young ladies."

"Why not?" Isobel demanded. "I can skate as good as Billy and Matt."

"As *well* as Billy and Matt," her mother corrected her.

Isobel heaved a frustrated sigh. "As *well* as Billy and Matt. So why shouldn't I be allowed to play?"

"You might get hurt," her father said. "Hockey is a rough sport."

"I'm not going to break, Papa. I'm fit and strong. Just yesterday I beat Billy at arm wrestling."

"I let you win," Billy blustered.

"You did not," Isobel retorted. "I beat you fair and square, Billy Harkness!"

"Children, stop," Mama said. "There will be no squabbling at the dinner table."

"And there will be no more arm wrestling either, Isobel," Papa added. He sent his daughter a look that meant the subject was closed. Then he turned to his wife. "It is obvious that Isobel is spending too much time with her brothers. Is there not something else she could do? Read poetry? Paint? Take singing lessons, perhaps?"

The mere thought made Isobel shudder. "Isobel Stanley plays hockey." She flung the words at her father like a dare. "I saw her picture in the newspaper. She plays with other young women on the rink at Rideau Hall. If the Governor General's daughter can play hockey, why can't I?"

"Isobel, that's quite enough," Mama scolded her.

Papa cleared his throat and picked up his knife and fork. "Listen to your mother, child. How Lord Stanley runs his family is his business. It has nothing to do with how I run mine. You may continue to skate, but there will be no more talk of hockey. Is that clear?"

Isobel scowled. It was clear all right. But she didn't have to like it.